Neil Gaiman is the ï author of the novels Aᵢ Boys, *Neverwhere, Corᵢ* Winner of the Hugo, Nᵢ his work has been adapted ιυr ɪɪɪm, television, and radio, including *Stardust* (2007) and the BAFTA-winning and Oscar-nominated animated feature film *Coraline* (2009). He has written scripts for *Doctor Who* and collaborated with Terry Pratchett and Chris Riddell, and *The Sandman* is already established as one of *the* classic graphic novels. As George R. R. Martin says, 'There's no one quite like Neil Gaiman.'

Praise for Neil Gaiman:

'His mind is a dark, fathomless ocean, and every time I sink into it, this world fades, replaced by one far more terrible and beautiful in which I will happily drown' *New York Times Book Review*

'He's the master of fantasy and realism twisted together' Hugo Rifkind, *Spectator*

'A very fine and imaginative writer' *The Sunday Times*

'A rich imagination . . . and an ability to tackle large themes' Philip Pullman

'Fantasy rooted in the darkest corners of reality' *Independent on Sunday*

'Gaiman is a master of fear, and he understands the nature of fairytales' A S Byatt, *Guardian*

By Neil Gaiman and available from Headline

Trigger Warning
The Ocean at the End of the Lane
Fragile Things
Anansi Boys
American Gods
Stardust
Smoke and Mirrors
Neverwhere

How the Marquis Got His Coat Back

The Truth is a Cave in the Black Mountains
(illustrated by Eddie Campbell)

MirrorMask: The Illustrated Film Script
(with Dave McKean)

NEIL GAIMAN

How The Marquis Got His Coat Back

headline

First published in *Rogues*, a short-story collection edited by George R. R. Martin and Gardner Dozois, in Great Britain in 2014 by Titan Books, a division of Titan Publishing Group Ltd.

This paperback edition published in 2015 by
HEADLINE PUBLISHING GROUP

16

Cataloguing in Publication Data is available from the British Library

ISBN 978 1 4722 3532 9

Typeset in Zapf Elliptical by Palimpsest Book Production Limited, Falkirk, Stirlingshire

Printed and bound in Great Britain by Clays Ltd, Elcograf S.p.A.

Headline's policy is to use papers that are natural, renewable and recyclable products and made from wood grown in sustainable forests. The logging and manufacturing processes are expected to conform to the environmental regulations of the country of origin.

HEADLINE PUBLISHING GROUP
An Hachette UK Company
Carmelite House
50 Victoria Embankment
London
EC4Y 0DZ

www.headline.co.uk
www.hachette.co.uk

How The Marquis
Got His Coat Back

It was beautiful. It was remarkable. It was unique. It was the reason that the Marquis de Carabas was chained to a pole in the middle of a circular room, far, far underground, while the water level rose slowly higher and higher. It had thirty pockets, seven of which were obvious, nineteen of which were hidden, and four of which were more or less impossible to find – even, on occasion, for the Marquis himself.

He had (we shall return to the pole, and the room, and the rising water, in due course) once been given – although 'given' might be considered an unfortunate, if justified, exaggeration

– a magnifying glass by Victoria herself. It was a marvellous piece of work: ornate, gilt, with a chain and tiny cherubs and gargoyles, and the lens had the unusual property of rendering transparent anything you looked at through it. The Marquis did not know where Victoria had originally obtained the magnifying glass, before he pilfered it from her, to make up for a payment he felt was not entirely what had been agreed – after all, there was only one Elephant, and obtaining the Elephant's diary had not been easy, nor had escaping the Elephant and Castle once it had been obtained. The Marquis had slipped Victoria's magnifying glass into one of the four pockets that practically weren't there at all and had never been able to find it again.

In addition to its unusual pockets, it had magnificent sleeves, an imposing collar, and a slit up the back. It was made of some kind of leather, it was the colour of a wet street at midnight, and, more important than any of these things, it had style.

There are people who will tell you that clothes

make the man, and mostly they are wrong. However, it would be true to say that when the boy who would become the Marquis put that coat on for the very first time, and stared at himself in the looking glass, he stood up straighter, and his posture changed, because he knew, seeing his reflection, that the sort of person who wore a coat like that was no mere youth, no simple sneak thief and favour-trader. The boy wearing the coat, which was, back then, too large for him, had smiled, looking at his reflection, and remembered an illustration from a book he had seen, of a miller's cat standing on its two hind legs. A jaunty cat wearing a fine coat and big, proud boots. And he named himself.

A coat like that, he knew, was the kind of coat that could only be worn by the Marquis de Carabas. He was never sure, not then and not later, how you pronounced Marquis de Carabas. Some days he said it one way, some days the other.

The water level had reached his knees, and he

thought, *This would never have happened if I still had my coat.*

It was the market day after the worst week of the Marquis de Carabas's life and things did not seem to be getting any better. Still, he was no longer dead, and his cut throat was healing rapidly. There was even a rasp in his throat he found quite attractive. Those were definite upsides.

There were just as definite downsides to being dead, or at least, to having been recently dead, and missing his coat was the worst of them.

The sewer folk were not helpful.

'You sold my corpse,' said the Marquis. 'These things happen. You also sold my possessions. I want them back. I'll pay.'

Dunnikin of the Sewer Folk shrugged. 'Sold them,' he said. 'Just like we sold you. Can't go getting things back that you sold. Not good business.'

'We are talking,' said the Marquis de Carabas, 'about my coat. And I fully intend to have it back.'

Dunnikin shrugged.

'To whom did you sell it?' asked the Marquis.

The Sewer dweller said nothing at all. He acted as if he had not even heard the question.

'I can get you perfumes,' said the Marquis, masking his irritability with all the blandness he could muster. 'Glorious, magnificent, odiferous perfumes. You know you want them.'

Dunnikin stared, stony-faced, at the Marquis. Then he drew his finger across his throat. As gestures went, the Marquis reflected, it was in appalling taste. Still, it had the desired effect. He stopped asking questions: there would be no answers from this direction.

The Marquis walked over to the food court. That night, the Floating Market was being held in the Tate Gallery. The food court was in the Pre-Raphaelite Room, and had already been mostly packed away. There were almost no stalls left: just a sad-looking little man selling some kind of sausage, and, in the corner, beneath a Burne-Jones painting of ladies in diaphanous robes walking downstairs, there were some

Mushroom People, with some stools, tables, and a grill. The Marquis had once eaten one of the sad-looking man's sausages, and he had a firm policy of never intentionally making the same mistake twice, so he walked to the Mushroom People's stall.

There were three of the Mushroom People looking after the stall, two young men and a young woman. They smelled damp. They wore old duffel coats and army-surplus jackets, and they peered out from beneath their shaggy hair as if the light hurt their eyes.

'What are you selling?' he asked.

'The Mushroom. The Mushroom on toast. Raw the Mushroom.'

'I'll have some of the Mushroom on toast,' he said, and one of the Mushroom People – a thin, pale young woman with the complexion of day-old porridge – cut a slice off a puffball fungus the size of a tree stump. 'And I want it cooked properly all the way through,' he told her.

'Be brave. Eat it raw,' said the woman. 'Join us.'

'I have already had dealings with the Mushroom,' said the Marquis. 'We came to an understanding.'

The woman put the slice of white puffball under the portable grill.

One of the young men, tall, with hunched shoulders, in a duffel coat that smelled like old cellars, edged over to the Marquis and poured him a glass of mushroom tea. He leaned forward, and the Marquis could see the tiny crop of pale mushrooms splashed like pimples over his cheek.

The Mushroom person said, 'You're de Carabas? The fixer?'

The Marquis did not think of himself as a fixer. He said, 'I am.'

'I hear you're looking for your coat. I was there when the Sewer Folk sold it. Start of the last Market it was. On Belfast. I saw who bought it.'

The hair on the back of the Marquis's neck pricked up. 'And what would you want for the information?'

The Mushroom's young man licked his lips

with a lichenous tongue. 'There's a girl I like as won't give me the time of day.'

'A Mushroom girl?'

'Would I were so lucky. If we were as one both in love and in the body of the Mushroom, I wouldn't have nothing to worry about. No. She's one of the Raven's Court. But she eats here sometimes. And we talk. Just like you and I are talking now.'

The Marquis did not smile in pity and he did not wince. He barely raised an eyebrow. 'And yet she does not return your ardor. How strange. What do you want me to do about it?'

The young man reached one grey hand into the pocket of his long duffel coat. He pulled out an envelope inside a clear plastic sandwich bag.

'I wrote her a letter. More of a poem, you might say, although I'm not much of a poet. To tell her how I feels about her. But I don't know that she'd read it if I gived it to her. Then I saw you, and I thought, if it was you as was to give it to her, with all your fine words and your fancy flourishes . . .' He trailed off.

'You thought she would read it and then be more inclined to listen to your suit.'

The young man looked down at his duffel coat with a puzzled expression. 'I've not got a suit,' he said. 'Only what I've got on.'

The Marquis tried not to sigh. The Mushroom woman put a cracked plastic plate down in front of him, with a steaming slice of grilled the Mushroom on it.

He poked at the Mushroom experimentally, making sure that it was cooked all the way through, and there were no active spores. You could never be too careful, and the Marquis considered himself much too selfish for symbiosis.

It was good. He chewed and swallowed, though the food hurt his throat.

'So all you want is for me to make sure she reads your missive of yearning?'

'You mean my letter? My poem?'

'I do.'

'Well, yes. And I want you to be there with her, to make sure she doesn't put it away unread, and I want you to bring her answer back to me.'

The Marquis looked at the young man. It was true that he had tiny mushrooms sprouting from his neck and cheeks, and his hair was heavy and unwashed, and there was a general smell about him of abandoned places, but it was also true that through his thick fringe his eyes were pale blue and intense, and that he was tall and not unattractive. The Marquis imagined him washed and cleaned up and somewhat less fungal, and approved. 'I put the letter in the sandwich bag,' said the young man, 'so it doesn't get wet on the way.'

'Very wise. Now, tell me: who bought my coat?'

'Not yet, Mister Jumps-the-Gun. You haven't asked about my true love. Her name is Drusilla. You'll know her because she is the most beautiful woman in all of the Raven's Court.'

'Beauty is traditionally in the eye of the beholder. Give me more to go on.'

'I told you. Her name's Drusilla. There's only one. And she has a big red birthmark on the back of her hand that looks like a star.'

'It seems an unlikely love pairing. One of the

Mushroom's folk, in love with a lady of the Raven's Court. What makes you think she'll give up her life for your damp cellars and fungoid joys?'

The Mushroom youth shrugged. 'She'll love me,' he said, 'once she's read my poem.' He twisted the stem of a tiny parasol mushroom growing on his right cheek and, when it fell to the table, he picked it up and continued to twist it between his fingers. 'We're on?'

'We're on.'

'The cove as bought your coat,' said the Mushroom youth, 'carried a stick.'

'Lots of people carry sticks,' said de Carabas.

'This one had a crook on the end,' said the Mushroom youth. 'Looked a bit like a frog, he did. Short one. Bit fat. Hair the colour of gravel. Needed a coat and took a shine to yours.' He popped the parasol mushroom into his mouth.

'Useful information. I shall certainly pass your ardour and felicitations on to the fair Drusilla,' said the Marquis de Carabas, with a cheer that he most definitely did not feel.

De Carabas reached across the table and took the sandwich bag with the envelope in it from the young man's fingers. He slipped it into one of the pockets sewn inside his shirt.

And then he walked away, thinking about a man holding a crook.

The Marquis de Carabas wore a blanket as a substitute for his coat. He wore it swathed about him like Hell's own poncho. It did not make him happy. He wished he had his coat. *Fine feathers do not make fine birds*, whispered a voice at the back of his mind, something someone had said to him when he was a boy: he suspected that it was his brother's voice, and he did his best to forget it had ever spoken.

A crook: the man who had taken his coat from the Sewer people had been carrying a crook.

He pondered.

The Marquis de Carabas liked being who he was, and when he took risks he liked them to be calculated risks, and he was someone who double- and triple-checked his calculations.

He checked his calculations for the fourth time.

The Marquis de Carabas did not trust people. It was bad for business and it could set an unfortunate precedent. He did not trust his friends or his occasional lovers, and he certainly never trusted his employers. He reserved the entirety of his trust for the Marquis de Carabas, an imposing figure in an imposing coat, able to outtalk, outthink, and outplan anybody.

There were only two sorts of people who carried crooks: bishops and shepherds.

In Bishopsgate, the crooks were decorative, nonfunctional, purely symbolic. And the bishops had no need of coats. They had robes, after all, nice, white, bishopy robes.

The Marquis was not scared of the bishops. He knew that the Sewer Folk were not scared of bishops. The inhabitants of Shepherd's Bush were another matter entirely. Even in his coat, and at the best of times, at the peak of health and with a small army at his beck and call, the Marquis would not have wanted to encounter the shepherds.

He toyed with the idea of visiting Bishopsgate, of spending a pleasant handful of days establishing that his coat was not there.

And then he sighed dramatically, and went to the Guide's Pen, and looked for a bonded guide who might be persuaded to take him to Shepherd's Bush.

His guide was quite remarkably short, with fair hair cut close. The Marquis had first thought she was in her teens, until, after travelling with her for half a day, he had decided she was in her twenties. He had talked to half a dozen guides before he found her. Her name was Knibbs, and she had seemed confident, and he needed confidence. He told her the two places he was going, as they walked out of the Guide's Pen.

'So where do you want to go first, then?' she asked. 'Shepherd's Bush, or Raven's Court?'

'The visit to Raven's Court is a formality: it is merely to deliver a letter. To someone named Drusilla.'

'A love letter?'

'I believe so. Why do you ask?'

'I have heard that the fair Drusilla is most wickedly beautiful, and she has the unfortunate habit of reshaping those who displease her into birds of prey. You must love her very much, to be writing letters to her.'

'I am afraid I have never encountered the young lady,' said the Marquis. 'The letter is not from me. And it doesn't matter which we visit first.'

'You know,' said Knibbs thoughtfully, 'just in case something dreadfully unfortunate happens to you when you get to the shepherds, we should probably do Raven's Court first. So the fair Drusilla gets her letter. I'm not saying that something horrible will happen to you, mind. Just that it's better to be safe than, y'know, dead.'

The Marquis de Carabas looked down at his blanketed shape. He was uncertain. Had he been wearing his coat, he knew, he would not have been uncertain: he would have known exactly what to do. He looked at the girl and he mustered the most convincing grin he could. 'Raven's Court it is, then,' he said.

Knibbs had nodded, and set off on the path, and the Marquis had followed her.

The paths of London Below are not the paths of London Above: they rely to no little extent on things like belief and opinion and tradition as much as they rely upon the realities of maps.

De Carabas and Knibbs were two tiny figures walking through a high, vaulted tunnel carved from old, white stone. Their footsteps echoed.

'You're de Carabas, aren't you?' said Knibbs. 'You're famous. You know how to get places. What exactly do you need a guide for?'

'Two heads are better than one,' he told her. 'So are two sets of eyes.'

'You used to have a posh coat, didn't you?' she said.

'*I* did. Yes.'

'What happened to it?'

He said nothing. Then he said, 'I've changed my mind. We're going to Shepherd's Bush first.'

'Fair enough,' said his guide. 'Easy to take you

one place as another. I'll wait for you outside the shepherds' trading post, mind.'

'Very wise, girl.'

'My name's Knibbs,' she said. 'Not girl. Do you want to know why I became a guide? It's an interesting story.'

'Not particularly,' said the Marquis de Carabas. He was not feeling particularly talkative, and the guide was being well recompensed for her trouble. 'Why don't we try to move in silence?'

Knibbs nodded and said nothing as they reached the end of the tunnel, nothing as they clambered down some metal rungs set in the side of a wall. It was not until they had reached the banks of the Mortlake, the vast underground Lake of the Dead, and she was lighting a candle on the shore to summon the boatman, that she spoke again.

Knibbs said, 'The thing about being a proper guide is that you're bonded. So people know you won't steer them wrong.'

The Marquis only grunted. He was wondering what to tell the shepherds at the trading post, trying out alternate routes through possibility

and through probability. He had nothing that
the shepherds would want, that was the trouble.

'You lead them wrong, you'll never work as a
guide again,' said Knibbs, cheerfully. 'That's
why we're bonded.'

'I know,' said the Marquis. She was a most
irritating guide, he thought. Two heads were
only better than one if the other head kept its
mouth shut and did not start telling him things
he already knew.

'I got bonded,' she said, 'in Bond Street.' She
tapped the little chain around her wrist.

'I don't see the ferryman,' said the Marquis.

'He'll be here soon enough. You keep an eye
out for him in that direction, and halloo when
you sees him. I'll keep looking over here. One
way or another, we'll spot him.'

They stared out over the dark water of the
Tyburn. Knibbs began to talk again. 'Before I
was a guide, when I was just little, my people
trained me up for this. They said it was the
only way that honor could ever be satisfied.'

The Marquis turned to face her. She held the

candle in front of her at eye level. *Everything is off here*, thought the Marquis, and he realised he should have been listening to her from the beginning. *Everything is wrong.* He said, 'Who are your people, Knibbs? Where do you come from?'

'Somewhere you ain't welcome anymore,' said the girl. 'I was born and bred to give my fealty and loyalty to the Elephant and the Castle.'

Something hard struck him on the back of the head then, hit him like a hammerblow, and lightning pulsed in the darkness of his mind as he crumpled to the floor.

The Marquis de Carabas could not move his arms. They were, he realised, tied behind him. He was lying on his side.

He had been unconscious. If the people who did this to him thought him unconscious still, then he would do nothing to disabuse them of the idea, he decided. He let his eyes slit open the merest crack, to sneak a glance at the world.

A deep, grinding voice said, 'Oh, don't be silly,

de Carabas. I don't believe you're still out. I've got big ears. I can hear your heart beat. Open your eyes properly, you weasel. Face me like a man.'

The Marquis recognised the voice and hoped he was mistaken. He opened his eyes. He was staring at legs, human legs with bare feet. The toes were squat and pushed together. The legs and feet were the colour of teak. He knew those legs. He had not been mistaken.

His mind bifurcated: a small part of it berated him for his inattention and his foolishness. Knibbs had *told* him, by the Temple and the Arch: he just had not listened to her. But even as he raged at his own foolishness, the rest of his mind took over, forced a smile, and said, 'Why, this is indeed an honour. You really didn't have to arrange to meet me like this. Why, the merest inkling that Your Prominence might have had even the teeniest desire to see me would have—'

'Sent you scurrying off in the other direction as fast as your spindly little legs could carry you,' said the person with the teak-coloured legs. He reached over with his trunk, which was long and flexible, and a greenish blue colour, and which hung to his ankles, and he pushed the Marquis on to his back.

The Marquis began rubbing his bound wrists slowly against the concrete beneath them while he said, 'Not at all. Quite the opposite. Words cannot actually describe how much pleasure I take in your pachydermic presence. Might I suggest that you untie me and allow me to greet you, man to . . . man to elephant?'

'I don't think so, given all the trouble I've been through to make this happen,' said the other. He had the head of a greenish grey elephant. His tusks were sharp and stained reddish brown at the tips. 'You know, I swore when I found out what you had done that I would make you scream and beg for mercy. And I swore I'd say no, to giving you mercy, when you begged for it.'

'You could say yes, instead,' said the Marquis.

'I couldn't say yes. Hospitality abused,' said the Elephant. 'I never forget.'

The Marquis had been commissioned to bring Victoria the Elephant's diary, when he and the world had been much younger. The Elephant ran his fiefdom arrogantly, sometimes viciously and with no tenderness or humor, and the Marquis had thought that the Elephant was stupid. He had even believed that there was no way that the Elephant would correctly identify his role in the disappearance of the diary. It had been a long time ago, though, when the Marquis was young and foolish.

'This whole spending years training up a guide to betray me just on the off chance I'd come along and hire her,' said the Marquis. 'Isn't that a bit of an overreaction?'

'Not if you know me,' said the Elephant. 'If you know me, it's pretty mild. I did lots of other things to find you too.'

The Marquis tried to sit up. The Elephant pushed him back to the floor with one bare foot. 'Beg for mercy,' said the Elephant.

That one was easy. 'Mercy!' said the Marquis. 'I beg! I plead! Show me mercy – the finest of all gifts. It befits you, mighty Elephant, as lord of your own demesne, to be merciful to one who is not even fit to wipe the dust from your excellent toes . . .'

'Did you know,' said the Elephant, 'that everything you say sounds sarcastic?'

'I didn't. I apologise. I meant every single word of it.'

'Scream,' said the Elephant.

The Marquis de Carabas screamed very loudly and very long. It is hard to scream when your throat has been recently cut, but he screamed as hard and piteously as he could.

'You even scream sarcastically,' said the Elephant.

There was a large black cast-iron pipe jutting out from the wall. A wheel in the side of the pipe allowed whatever came out of the pipe to be turned on and turned off. The Elephant hauled on it with powerful arms, and a trickle of dark sludge came out, followed by a spurt of water.

'Drainage overflow,' said the Elephant. 'Now.

Thing is, I do my homework. You keep your life well hidden, de Carabas. You have done all these years, since you and I first crossed paths. No point in even trying anything as long as you had your life elsewhere. I've had people all over London Below: people you've eaten with, people you've slept with or laughed with or wound up naked in the clock tower of Big Ben with, but there was never any point in taking it further, not as long as your life was still carefully tucked out of harm's way. Until last week, when the word under the street was that your life was out of its box. And that was when I put the word out, that I'd give the freedom of the Castle to the first person to let me see . . .'

'. . . See me scream for mercy,' said de Carabas. 'You said.'

'You interrupted me,' said the Elephant mildly. 'I was going to say, I was going to give the freedom of the Castle to the first person to let me see your dead body.'

He pulled the wheel the rest of the way and the spurt of water became a gush.

'I ought to warn you. There is,' said de Carabas, 'a curse on the hand of anyone who kills me.'

'I'll take the curse,' said the Elephant. 'Although you're probably making it up. You'll like the next bit. The room fills with water, and then you drown. Then I let the water out, and I come in, and I laugh a lot.' He made a trumpeting noise that might, de Carabas reflected, have been a laugh, if you were an elephant.

The Elephant stepped out of de Carabas's line of sight.

The Marquis heard a door bang. He was lying in a puddle. He writhed and wriggled, then got to his feet. He looked down: there was a metal cuff around his ankle, which was chained to a metal pole in the center of the room.

He wished he were wearing his coat: there were blades in his coat; there were picklocks; there were buttons that were nowhere nearly as innocent and buttonlike as they appeared to be. He rubbed the rope that bound his wrists against the metal pole, hoping to make it fray, feeling the skin of his wrists and palms rubbing off even as the rope absorbed the water and tightened about him. The water level continued to rise: already it was up to his waist.

De Carabas looked about the circular chamber. All he had to do was free himself from the bonds that tied his wrists – obviously by loosening the pole to which he was bound – and then he would open the cuff around his ankle, turn off the water, get out of the room, avoid a revenge-driven Elephant and any of his assorted thugs, and get away.

He tugged on the pole. It didn't move. He tugged on it harder. It didn't move some more.

He slumped against the pole, and he thought about death, a true, final death, and he thought about his coat.

A voice whispered in his ear. It said, 'Quiet!'

Something tugged at his wrists, and his bonds fell away. It was only as life came back into his wrists that he realised how tightly he had been bound. He turned around.

He said, 'What?'

The face that met his was as familiar as his

own. The smile was devastating, the eyes were guileless and adventuresome.

'Ankle,' said the man, with a new smile that was even more devastating than the previous one.

The Marquis de Carabas was not devastated. He raised his leg, and the man reached down, did something with a piece of wire, and removed the leg cuff.

'I heard you were having a spot of bother,' said the man. His skin was as dark as the Marquis's own. He was less than an inch taller than de Carabas, but he held himself as if he were easily taller than anyone he was ever likely to meet.

'No. No bother. I'm fine,' said the Marquis.

'You aren't. I just rescued you.'

De Carabas ignored this. 'Where's the Elephant?'

'On the other side of that door, with a number of the people working for him. The doors lock automatically when the hall is filled with water. He needed to be certain that he wouldn't be trapped in here with you. It was what I was counting on.'

'Counting on?'

'Of course. I'd been following them for several hours. Ever since I heard that you'd gone off with one of the Elephant's plants. I thought, bad move, I thought. He'll be needing a hand with that.'

'You *heard* . . . ?'

'Look,' said the man who looked a little like the Marquis de Carabas, only he was taller, and perhaps some people – not the Marquis, obviously – might have thought him just a hair better-looking, 'you don't think I was going to let anything happen to my little brother, did you?'

They were up to their waists in water. 'I was fine,' said de Carabas. 'I had it all under control.'

The man walked over to the far end of the room. He knelt down, fumbled in the water, then, from his backpack, he produced something that looked like a short crowbar. He pushed one end of it beneath the surface of the water. 'Get ready,' he said. 'I think this should be our quickest way out of here.'

The Marquis was still flexing his pins-and-needles cramping fingers, trying to rub life back into them. 'What is it?' he said, trying to sound unimpressed.

The man said, 'There we go,' and pulled up a large square of metal. 'It's the drain.' De Carabas did not have a chance to protest, as his brother picked him up and dropped him down a hole in the floor.

Probably, thought de Carabas, *there are rides like this at funfairs*. He could imagine them. Upworlders might pay good money to take this ride if they were certain they would survive it.

He crashed through pipes, swept along by the flow of water, always heading down and deeper. He was not certain he was going to survive it, and he was not having fun.

The Marquis's body was bruised and battered as he rode the water down the pipe. He tumbled out, facedown, onto a large metal grate, which seemed scarcely able to hold his weight. He crawled off the grate on to the rock floor beside it, and he shivered.

There was an unlikely sort of a noise, and it

was immediately followed by his brother, who shot out of the pipe and landed on his feet, as if he'd been practising. He smiled. 'Fun, eh?'

'Not really,' said the Marquis de Carabas. And then he had to ask. 'Were you just going "*Whee!*"?'

'Of course! Weren't you?' asked his brother.

De Carabas got to his feet, unsteadily. He said only, 'What are you calling yourself these days?'

'Still the same. I don't change.'

'It's not your real name, Peregrine,' said de Carabas.

'It'll do. It marks my territory and my intentions. You're still calling yourself a Marquis, then?' said Peregrine.

'I am, because I say I am,' said the Marquis. He looked, he was sure, like a drowned thing, and sounded, he was certain, unconvincing. He felt small and foolish.

'Your choice. Anyway, I'm off. You don't need me anymore. Stay out of trouble. You don't actually have to thank me.' His brother meant it, of course. That was what stung the hardest.

The Marquis de Carabas hated himself. He

hadn't wanted to say it, but now it had to be said. 'Thank you, Peregrine.'

'Oh!' said Peregrine. 'Your coat. Word on the street is, it wound up in Shepherd's Bush. That's all I know. So. Advice. Mean this most sincerely. I know you don't like advice. But, the coat? Let it go. Forget about it. Just get a new coat. Honest.'

'Well then,' said the Marquis.

'Well,' said Peregrine, and he grinned and shook himself like a dog, spraying water everywhere, before he slipped into the shadows and was gone.

The Marquis de Carabas stood and dripped balefully.

He had a little time before the Elephant discovered the lack of water in the room, and the lack of a body, and came looking for him.

He checked his shirt pocket: the sandwich bag was there, and the envelope appeared safe and dry inside it.

He wondered, for a moment, about something that had bothered him since the Market. Why would the Mushroom lad use him, de Carabas, to send a letter to the fair Drusilla? And what

kind of letter could persuade a member of the
Raven's Court, and one with a star on her hand
at that, to give up her life at the court and love
one of the Mushroom People?

A suspicion occurred to him. It was not a
comfortable idea, but it was swept aside by
more immediate problems.

He could hide: lie low for a while. It would pass.
But there was the coat to think about. He had been
rescued – rescued! – by his brother, something
that would never have happened under normal
circumstances. He could get a new coat. Of course
he could. But it would not be *his* coat.

A shepherd had his coat.

The Marquis de Carabas always had a plan,
and he always had a fallback plan; and beneath
these plans he always had a real plan, one that
he would not even let himself know about, for
when the original plan and the fallback plan
had both gone south.

Now, it pained him to admit to himself, he had
no plan. He did not even have a normal, boring,
obvious plan that he could abandon as soon as

things got tricky. He just had a *want*, and it drove him as their need for food or love or safety drove those the Marquis considered lesser men.

He was planless. He just wanted his coat back.

The Marquis de Carabas began walking. He had an envelope containing a love poem in his pocket, he was wrapped in a damp blanket, and he hated his brother for rescuing him.

When you create yourself from scratch you need a model of some kind, something to aim towards or head away from – all the things you want to be, or intentionally not be.

The Marquis had known whom he had wanted not to be, when he was a boy. He had definitely not wanted to be like Peregrine. He had not wanted to be like anyone at all. He had, instead, wanted to be elegant, elusive, brilliant and, above all things, he had wanted to be unique.

Just like Peregrine.

The thing was, he had been told by a former shepherd on the run, whom he had helped across the Tyburn River to freedom, and to a short but happy life as a camp entertainer for the Roman Legion who waited there, beside the river, for orders that would never come, that the shepherds never *made* you do anything. They just took your natural impulses and desires and they pushed them, reinforced them, so you acted quite naturally, only you acted in the ways that they wanted.

He remembered that, and then he forgot it, because he was scared of being alone.

The Marquis had not known until just this moment quite how scared he was of being alone, and was surprised by how happy he was to see several other people walking in the same direction as he was.

'I'm glad you're here,' one of them called.

'I'm glad you're here,' called another.

'I'm glad I'm here too,' said de Carabas. Where was he going? Where were they going? So good that they were all traveling the same way together. There was safety in numbers.

'It's good to be together,' said a thin white woman, with a happy sort of a sigh. And it was.

'It's good to be together,' said the Marquis.

'Indeed it is. It's good to be together,' said his neighbor on the other side. There was something familiar about this person. He had huge ears, like fans, and a nose like a thick, grey-green snake. The Marquis began to wonder if he had ever met this person before, and was trying to remember exactly where, when he was tapped gently on the shoulder by a man holding a large stick with a curved end.

'We never want to fall out of step, do we?' said the man, reasonably, and the Marquis thought *Of course we don't*, and he sped up a little, so he was back in step once more.

'That's good. Out of step is out of mind,' said the man with the stick, and he moved on.

'Out of step is out of mind,' said the Marquis aloud, wondering how he could have missed knowing something so obvious, so basic. There was a tiny part of him, somewhere distant, that wondered what that actually meant.

They reached the place they were going, and it was good to be among friends.

Time passed strangely in that place, but soon

enough the Marquis and his friend with the grey-green face and the long nose were given a job to do, a real job, and it was this: they disposed of those members of the flock who could no longer move or serve, once anything that might be of use had been removed and reused. They removed the last of what was left, hair and tallow fat and all, then they dragged it to the pit, and dropped the remnants in. The shifts were long and tiring, and the work was messy, but the two of them did it together and they stayed in step.

They had been working proudly together for several days when the Marquis noticed an irritant. Someone appeared to be trying to attract his attention.

'I followed you,' whispered the stranger. 'I know you didn't want me to. But, well, needs must.'

The Marquis did not know what the stranger was talking about.

'I've got an escape plan, as soon as I can wake you up,' said the stranger. 'Please wake up.'

The Marquis was awake. Again, he found he did not know what the stranger was talking about. Why did the man think he was asleep? The Marquis would have said something, but he had to work. He pondered this, while dismembering the next former member of the flock, until he decided there was something he could say, to explain why the stranger was irritating him. He said it aloud. 'It's good to work,' said the Marquis.

His friend, with the long, flexible nose, and the huge ears, nodded his head at this.

They worked. After a while his friend hauled what was left of some former members of the flock over to the pit, and pushed them in. The pit went down a long way.

The Marquis tried to ignore the stranger, who was now standing behind him. He was quite put out when he felt something slapped over his mouth, and his hands being bound together behind his back. He was not certain what he was meant to do. It made him feel quite out of step with the flock, and he would have complained, would have called out to his friend, but his lips were now stuck together and he was unable to do more than make ineffectual noises.

'It's me,' whispered the voice from behind him urgently. 'Peregrine. Your brother. You've been captured by the shepherds. We have to get you out of here.' And then: 'Uh-uh.'

A noise in the air, like something barking. It came closer: a high yip-yipping that turned suddenly into a triumphant howl, and was answered by matching howls from around them.

A voice barked, 'Where's your flockmate?'

A low, elephantine voice rumbled, 'He went over there. With the other one.'

'Other one?'

The Marquis hoped they would come and find him and sort this all out. There was obviously some sort of mistake going on. He wanted to be in step with the flock, and now he was out of step, an unwilling victim. He wanted to work.

'Lud's gate!' muttered Peregrine. And then they were surrounded by shapes of people who were not exactly people: they were sharp of face and dressed in furs. They spoke excitedly to one another.

The people untied the Marquis's hands, although they left the tape on his face. He did not mind. He had nothing to say.

The Marquis was relieved it was all over and looked forward to getting back to work, but to his slight puzzlement, he, his kidnapper, and his friend with the huge, long, flexible nose were walked away from the pit, along a causeway, and eventually, into a honeycomb of little rooms, each room filled with people toiling away in step.

Up some narrow stairs. One of their escorts, dressed in rough furs, scratched at a door. A voice called 'Enter!' and the Marquis felt a thrill that was almost sexual. That voice. That was the voice of someone the Marquis had spent his whole life wanting to please. (His whole life went back, what? A week? Two weeks?)

'A stray lamb,' said one of the escorts. 'And his predator. Also his flockmate.'

The room was large, and hung with oil paintings: landscapes, mostly, stained with age and smoke and dust. 'Why?' said the man, sitting at a desk in the back of the room. He did not turn around. 'Why do you bother me with this nonsense?'

'Because,' said a voice, and the Marquis recognised it as that of his would-be kidnapper, 'you gave orders that if ever I were to be apprehended within the bounds of the Shepherd's Bush, I was to be brought to you to dispose of personally.'

The man pushed his chair back and got up. He walked towards them, stepping into the light. There was a wooden crook propped against the wall, and he picked it up as he passed. For several long moments he looked at them.

'Peregrine?' he said at last, and the Marquis thrilled at his voice. 'I had heard that you had gone into retirement. Become a monk or something. I never dreamed you'd dare to come back.'

(Something very big was filling the Marquis's head. Something was filling his heart and his mind. It was something enormous, something he could almost touch.)

The shepherd reached out a hand and ripped the tape from the Marquis's mouth. The Marquis knew he should have been overjoyed by this, should have been thrilled to get attention from this man.

'And now I see . . . who would have thought it?' The shepherd's voice was deep and resonant. 'He is here already. And already one of ours? The Marquis de Carabas. You know, Peregrine, I had been looking forward to ripping out your tongue, to grinding your fingers away while you watched, but think how much more delightful it would be if the last thing you ever saw was your own brother, one of our flock, as the instrument of your doom.'

(An enormous thing filled the Marquis's head.)

The shepherd was plump, well fed, and excellently dressed. He had sandy-grey-coloured hair and a harassed expression. He wore a remarkable coat, even if it was somewhat tight on him. The coat was the colour of a wet street at midnight.

The enormous thing filling his head, the Marquis realised, was rage. It was rage, and it burned through the Marquis like a forest fire, devouring everything in its path with a red flame.

The coat. It was elegant. It was beautiful. It was so close that he could have reached out and touched it.

And it was unquestionably *his*.

The Marquis de Carabas did nothing to indicate that he had woken up. That would be a mistake. He thought, and he thought fast. And what he thought had nothing to do with the room he was in. The Marquis had only one advantage over the shepherd and his dogs: he knew he was awake and in control of his thoughts, and they did not.

He hypothesised. He tested his hypothesis in his head. And then he acted.

'Excuse me,' he said blandly, 'but I'm afraid I do need to be getting along. Can we hurry this up? I'm late for something that's frightfully important.'

The shepherd leaned on his crook. He did not

appear to be concerned by this. He said only, 'You've left the flock, de Carabas.'

'It would appear so,' said the Marquis. 'Hello, Peregrine. Wonderful to see you looking so sprightly. And the Elephant. How delightful. The gang's all here.' He turned his attention back to the shepherd. 'Wonderful meeting you, delightful to spend a little time as one of your little band of serious thinkers. But I really must be tootling off now. Important diplomatic mission. Letter to deliver. You know how it is.'

Peregrine said, 'My brother, I'm not sure that you understand the gravity of the situation here . . .'

The Marquis, who understood the gravity of the situation perfectly, said, 'I'm sure these nice people' – he gestured to the shepherd and to the three fur-clad, sharp-faced, sheepdog people who were standing about them – 'will let me head out of here, leaving you behind. It's you they want, not me. And I have something extremely important to deliver.'

Peregrine said, 'I can handle this.'

'You have to be quiet now,' said the shepherd. He took the strip of tape he had removed from the Marquis's mouth and pressed it down over Peregrine's.

The shepherd was shorter than the Marquis and fatter, and the magnificent coat looked faintly ridiculous on him. 'Something important to deliver?' asked the shepherd, brushing dust from his fingers. 'What exactly are we talking about here?'

'I am afraid I cannot possibly tell you that,' said the Marquis. 'You are, after all, not the intended recipient of this particular diplomatic communiqué.'

'Why not? What's it say? Who's it for?'

The Marquis shrugged. His coat was so close that he could have reached out and stroked it. 'Only the threat of death could force me even to show it to you,' he said reluctantly.

'Well, that's easy. I threaten you with death. That's in addition to the death sentence you're already under as an apostate member of the flock. And as for Laughing Boy here' – the shepherd gestured with his crook towards Peregrine, who was not laughing – 'he's tried to steal a member of the flock. That's a death sentence too, in addition to everything else we're planning to do to him.'

The shepherd looked at the Elephant. 'And, I know I should have asked before, but what in the Auld Witch's name is this?'

'I am a loyal member of the flock,' said the Elephant humbly, in his deep voice, and the Marquis wondered if he had sounded so soulless and flat when he had been part of the flock. 'I have remained loyal and in step even when this one did not.'

'And the flock is grateful for all your hard work,' said the shepherd. He reached out a hand and touched the sharp tip of one elephantine tusk experimentally. 'I've never seen anything like you before, and if I never see another one again, it'll be too soon. Probably best if you die too.'

The Elephant's ears twitched. 'But I am of the flock . . .'

The shepherd looked up into the Elephant's

huge face. 'Better safe than sorry,' he said. Then, to the Marquis: 'Well? Where is this important letter?'

The Marquis de Carabas said, 'It is inside my shirt. I must repeat that it is the most significant document that I have ever been charged to deliver. I must ask you not to look at it. For your own safety.'

The shepherd tugged at the front of the Marquis's shirt. The buttons flew, and rattled off the walls on to the floor. The letter, in its sandwich bag, was in the pocket inside the shirt.

'This is most unfortunate. I trust you will read it aloud to us before we die,' said the Marquis. 'But whether or not you read it to us, I can promise that Peregrine and I will be holding our breath. Won't we, Peregrine?'

The shepherd opened the sandwich bag, then he looked at the envelope. He ripped it open and pulled a sheet of discoloured paper from inside it. Dust came from the envelope as the paper came out. The dust hung in the still air in that dim room.

'"My darling beautiful Drusilla,"' read the

shepherd aloud. '"While I know that you do not presently feel about me as I feel about you . . ." what *is* this nonsense?'

The Marquis said nothing. He did not even smile. He was, as he had stated, holding his breath; he was hoping that Peregrine had listened to him; and he was counting, because at that moment counting seemed like the best possible thing that he could do to distract himself from needing to breathe. He would soon need to breathe.

35 . . . 36 . . . 37 . . .

He wondered how long mushroom spores remained in the air.

43 . . . 44 . . . 45 . . . 46 . . .

The shepherd had stopped speaking.

The Marquis took a step backwards, fearing a knife in his ribs or teeth in his throat from the rough-furred guard-dog men, but there was nothing. He walked backwards, away from the dog-men, and the Elephant.

He saw that Peregrine was also walking backwards.

His lungs hurt. His heart was pounding in his temples, pounding almost loudly enough to drown out the thin ringing noise in his ears.

Only when the Marquis's back was against a bookcase on the wall and he was as far as he could possibly get from the envelope, he allowed himself to take a deep breath. He heard Peregrine breathe in too.

There was a stretching noise. Peregrine opened his mouth wide, and the tape dropped to the ground. 'What,' asked Peregrine, 'was all that about?'

'Our way out of this room, and our way out of Shepherd's Bush, if I am not mistaken,' said de Carabas. 'As I so rarely am. Would you mind unbinding my wrists?'

He felt Peregrine's hands on his bound hands, and then the bindings fell away.

There was a low rumbling. 'I'm going to kill somebody,' said the Elephant. 'As soon as I figure out who.'

'Whoa, dear heart,' said the Marquis, rubbing his hands together. 'You mean *whom*.' The shepherd and the sheepdogs were taking awkward, experimental steps towards the door. 'And I can assure you that you aren't going to kill anybody, not as long as you want to get home to the Castle safely.'

The Elephant's trunk swished irritably. 'I'm definitely going to kill *you*.'

The Marquis grinned. 'You are going to force me to say *pshaw*,' he said. 'Or *fiddlesticks*. Until now I have never had the slightest moment of yearning to say *fiddlesticks*. But I can feel it right now welling up inside me—'

'What, by the Temple and the Arch, has got into you?' asked the Elephant.

'Wrong question. But I shall ask the right question on your behalf. The question is actually what *hasn't* got into the three of us – it hasn't got into Peregrine and me because we were holding our breath, and it hasn't got into you because, I don't know, probably because you're an elephant, with nice thick skin, more likely because you were breathing through your trunk, which is down at ground level – and what did get into our captors.

And the answer is, what hasn't got into us are the selfsame spores that have got into our portly shepherd and his pseudocanine companions.'

'Spores of the Mushroom?' asked Peregrine. 'The Mushroom People's the Mushroom?'

'Indeed. That selfsame Mushroom,' agreed the Marquis.

'Blimming Heck,' said the Elephant.

'Which is why,' de Carabas told the Elephant, 'if you attempt to kill me, or to kill Peregrine, you will not only fail but you will doom us all. Whereas if you shut up and we all do our best to look as if we are still part of the flock, then we have a chance. The spores will be threading their way into their brains now. And any moment now the Mushroom will begin calling them home.'

A shepherd walked implacably. He held a wooden crook. Three men followed him. One of those men had the head of an elephant; one was tall and ridiculously handsome; and the last of the flock wore a most magnificent coat. It fit him perfectly, and it was the colour of a wet street at night.

The flock were followed by guard dogs, who moved as if they were ready to walk through fire to get wherever they believed that they were going.

It was not unusual in Shepherd's Bush to see a shepherd and part of his flock moving from place to place, accompanied by several of the fiercest sheepdogs (who were human, or had been once). So when they saw a shepherd and three sheepdogs apparently leading three members of the flock away from Shepherd's Bush, none of the greater flock paid them any mind. The members of the flock who saw them simply did the same things they had always done, as members of the flock, and if they were aware that the influence of the shepherds had waned a little, then they patiently waited for another shepherd to come and to take care of them and to keep them safe from predators and from the world. It was a scary thing to be alone, after all.

Nobody noticed as they crossed the bounds of Shepherd's Bush, and still they kept on walking.

The seven of them reached the banks of the Kilburn, where they stopped, and the former shepherd and the three shaggy dog-men strode out into the water.

There was, the Marquis knew, nothing in the four men's heads at that moment but a need to get to the Mushroom, to taste its flesh once more, to let it live inside them, to serve it, and to serve it well. In exchange, the Mushroom would fix all the things about themselves that they hated: it would make their interior lives much happier and more interesting.

'Should've let me kill 'em,' said the Elephant as the former shepherd and sheepdogs waded away.

'No point,' said the Marquis. 'Not even for revenge. The people who captured us don't exist any longer.'

The Elephant flapped his ears hard, then scratched them vigorously. 'Talking about revenge, who the hell did you steal my diary for anyway?' he asked.

'Victoria,' admitted de Carabas.

'Not actually on my list of potential thieves.

She's a deep one,' said the Elephant, after a moment.

'I'll not argue with that,' said the Marquis. 'Also, she failed to pay me the entire amount agreed. I wound up obtaining my own *lagniappe* to make up the deficit.'

He reached a dark hand into the inside of his coat. His fingers found the obvious pockets, and the less obvious, and then to his surprise, the least obvious of all. He reached inside it and pulled out a magnifying glass on a chain. 'It was Victoria's,' he said. 'I believe you can use it to see through solid things. Perhaps this could be considered a small payment against my debt to you . . .?'

The Elephant took something out of its own pocket – the Marquis could not see what it was – and squinted at it through the magnifying glass. Then the Elephant made a noise halfway between a delighted snort and a trumpet of satisfaction. 'Oh fine, very fine,' it said. It pocketed both of the objects. Then it said, 'I suppose that saving my life outranks stealing my diary. And while I wouldn't have needed saving if I hadn't followed you down the drain, further recriminations are pointless. Consider your life your own once more.'

'I look forward to visiting you in the Castle someday,' said the Marquis.

'Don't push your luck, mate,' said the Elephant, with an irritable swish of his trunk.

'I won't,' said the Marquis, resisting the urge to point out that pushing his luck was the only way he had made it this far. He looked around and realised that Peregrine had slipped mysteriously and irritatingly away into the shadows, once more, without so much as a goodbye.

The Marquis hated it when people did that.

He made a small, courtly bow to the Elephant, and the Marquis's coat, his glorious coat, caught the bow, amplified it, made it perfect, and made it the kind of bow that only the Marquis de Carabas could ever possibly make. Whoever he was.

The next Floating Market was being held in Derry and Tom's Roof Garden. There had been no Derry and Tom's since 1973, but time and space and London Below had their own uncomfortable agreement, and the roof garden was younger and more innocent than it is today. The folk from London Above (they were young, and in an intense discussion, and they had stacked heels and paisley tops and bell-bottom flares, the men and the women) ignored the folk from London Below entirely.

The Marquis de Carabas strode through the roof garden as if he owned the place, walking swiftly until he reached the food court. He passed a tiny woman selling curling cheese sandwiches from a wheelbarrow piled high with the things, a curry stall, a short man with a huge glass bowl of pale white blind fish and a toasting fork, until, finally, he reached the stall that was selling the Mushroom.

'Slice of the Mushroom, well grilled, please,' said the Marquis de Carabas.

The man who took his order was shorter than he was and still somewhat stouter. He had sandy, receding hair and a harried expression.

'Coming right up,' said the man. 'Anything else?'

'No, that's all.' And then, curiously, the Marquis asked, 'Do you remember me?'

'I am afraid not,' said the Mushroom man. 'But I must say, that is a most beautiful coat.'

'Thank you,' said the Marquis de Carabas. He looked around. 'Where is the young fellow who used to work here?'

'Ah. That is a most curious story, sir,' said the man. He did not yet smell of damp although there was a small encrustation of mushrooms on the side of his neck. 'Somebody told the fair Drusilla, of the Court of the Raven, that our Vince had had designs upon her, and had – you may not credit it, but I am assured that it is so – apparently sent her a letter filled with spores with the intention of making her his bride in the Mushroom.'

The Marquis raised an eyebrow quizzically, although he found none of this surprising. He had, after all, told Drusilla himself, and had even shown her the original letter. 'Did she take well to the news?'

'I do not believe that she did, sir. I do not believe that she did. She and several of her sisters were waiting for Vince, and they all caught up with us on our way to the Market. She told him they had matters to discuss, of an intimate nature. He seemed delighted by this news, and went off with her to find out what these matters were. I have been waiting for him to arrive at the Market and come and work all evening, but I no longer believe he will be coming.' Then the man said a little wistfully, 'That is a very fine coat. It seems to me that I might have had one like it in a former life.'

'I do not doubt it,' said the Marquis de Carabas, satisfied with what he had heard, cutting into his grilled slice of the Mushroom, 'but this particular coat is most definitely mine.'

As he made his way out of the Market, he passed a clump of people descending the stairs and he paused and nodded at a young woman of uncommon grace. She had the long orange hair and the flattened profile of a Pre-Raphaelite beauty, and there was a birthmark in the shape of a five-pointed star on the back of one hand. Her other hand was stroking the head of a large, rumpled owl, which glared uncomfortably out at the world with eyes that were, unusually for such a bird, of an intense, pale blue.

The Marquis nodded at her, and she glanced awkwardly at him, then she looked away in the manner of someone who was now beginning to realise that she owed the Marquis a favour.

He nodded at her amiably, and continued to descend.

Drusilla hurried after him. She looked as if she had something she wanted to say.

The Marquis de Carabas reached the foot of the stairs ahead of her. He stopped for a moment, and he thought about people, and about things, and about how hard it is to do anything for the first time. And then, clad in his fine coat, he slipped mysteriously, even irritatingly, into the shadows, without so much as a goodbye, and he was gone.